THE MOVIE
STORYBOOK

COLUMBIA PICTURES PRESENTS A MARVEL ENTERPRISES / LAURA ZISKIN PRODUCTION
TOBEY MAGUIRE "SPIDER-MAN" 2" KIRSTEN DUNST JAMES FRANCO ALFRED MOLINA ROSEMARY HARRIS DONNA MURPHY
MUSIC BY DANNY ELFMAN EXECUTIVE PRODUCERS STAN LEE KEVIN FEIGE EXECUTIVE PRODUCER JOSEPH M. CARACCIOLO BASED ON THE MARVEL COMIC BOOK BY STAN LEE AND STEVE DITKO
SCREEN STORY BY ALFRED GOUGH & MILES MILLAR AND MICHAEL CHABON SCREENPLAY BY ALVIN SARGENT PRODUCED BY LAURA ZISKIN AVI ARAD DIRECTED BY SAM RAIMI

MARVEL   SPIDER-MAN CHARACTER ® & © 2004 MARVEL CHARACTERS, INC. ALL RIGHTS RESERVED.   sony.com/Spider-Man   DISTRIBUTED BY COLUMBIA TRISTAR FILM DISTRIBUTORS INTERNATIONAL

Spider-Man 2: The Movie Storybook
Spider-Man and all related characters: ™ & © 2004 Marvel Characters, Inc.
Spider-Man 2, the movie: © 2004 Columbia Pictures Industries, Inc.
All Rights Reserved.
Photos by Melissa Moseley.
Photos on pages 29, 31, 37, and 48 by Sony Pictures Imageworks
First published in the USA by HarperFestival in 2004
First published in Great Britain by HarperCollins*Entertainment* in 2004
HarperCollins*Entertainment* is an imprint of HarperCollins Publishers Ltd,
77-85 Fulham Palace Road, Hammersmith, London W6 8JB

135798642
ISBN 0-00-717814-X

Printed and bound in the UK

www.harpercollinschildrensbooks.co.uk
www.sony.com/Spider-Man

SPIDER-MAN 2

THE MOVIE STORYBOOK

Adapted by Kate Egan
Based on the Motion Picture
Screenplay by Alvin Sargent
Screen Story by
Alfred Gough & Miles Millar
and Michael Chabon
Based on the Marvel Comic Book
by Stan Lee and Steve Ditko

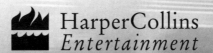

HarperCollins
Entertainment

An imprint of HarperCollins*Publishers*

Meet Peter Parker. Meet Spider-Man. Peter and Spider-Man are the same person. No one knows that except for Peter. Keeping such a big secret is not easy.

Peter has been having a lot of trouble with life. He couldn't convince J. J. Jameson, his boss at the *Daily Bugle*, to buy his photographs of New York. Jameson only wanted pictures of Spider-Man.

Then at school, Peter ran straight into his professor, Dr. Connors.

"Where are you headed, Parker?" Dr. Connors asked.

"To your class."

"Peter, my class is over. What's up with you these days? You're late all the time, your grades are going down, and you still owe me a paper. If things don't change, you're going to fail my class."

Peter looked at his watch and took off. He was even late for his own birthday party! Dr. Connors was right. Peter needed to get his act together.

When he reached Aunt May's house, the other guests had already arrived. His good friend and next-door neighbor, Mary Jane Watson, was there. So was his best friend, Harry Osborn.

While Peter was struggling with his dual lives, his friends were getting ahead. He heard their good news at the party. Mary Jane had always dreamed of becoming an actress. Now she had a part in an off-Broadway show! Harry was living his dream, too. He was carrying on his father's work at OsCorp, the company his dad had founded. He told Peter about one of the company's latest projects: funding an experiment of Dr. Otto Octavius.

"I'm writing a paper on him," Peter told Harry.

Harry invited Peter to meet Dr. Octavius at an upcoming demonstration. Peter could hardly wait. Dr. Octavius was one of his idols.

M. J. stood up from the table. "Well, it's time for me to go if I want to be at the theater on time."

Harry said, "I'll give you a ride, M. J. I've got to get back to the city, too."

"I'll be at the show tonight, M. J.," Peter said. "I can't wait to see it."

M. J. looked at him as if she didn't believe a word he was saying. True, he hadn't been all that reliable lately. But there was no way he would miss this.

After joining Aunt May for birthday cake and tea, Peter stood to go. He didn't want to be late.

Peter hopped on his motorbike and set off for Manhattan. When he was near the theater, he stopped to buy flowers for M. J. Just as he took his change and headed back to his bike, his spider sense kicked in. Then several gunshots rang out, and a speeding car raced by him.

Peter ran into an alley and changed into his Spider-Man suit.

Spider-Man emerged from the alley and jumped onto the racing car. He dodged the villains' bullets and quickly surrounded the two men with a web, yanking them out of their car and tying them to a lamppost.

Quickly, he changed back into his regular clothes. Uh, oh. He was going to be late for M. J.'s play. He hopped into the beat-up convertible that the villains had been driving and sped off to the theater.

When Peter arrived, the theater doors were closed. The play had already started. Inside the theater, M. J. looked out into the audience and saw an empty seat where Peter should have been. She knew it! He had disappointed her again.

Peter returned home, frustrated. Being a hero was definitely interfering with his personal life. If only he could tell M. J. about being Spider-Man, then she would understand everything.

The next day, Peter called M. J. to apologize for missing the play. She didn't pick up the phone. She had clearly had enough of Peter's excuses.

At last, the day of Dr. Otto Octavius's demonstration had arrived. The lab was packed with famous scientists. From the corner where he stood with Harry, Peter watched Dr. Octavius reveal a machine with octopus-like arms. The arms were connected to a harness. Dr. Octavius strapped the contraption onto his body and explained that the "smart arms" were constructed to aid humans in multitasking or working in dangerous conditions.

"Just think," the scientist said, "a lead surgeon could now perform surgery all by himself. Workers will never have to personally handle radioactive materials. The uses are limitless!"

Dr. Octavius began to demonstrate various tasks the arms could perform. At first the experiment was a tremendous success. After a few minutes, the arms started to malfunction. Dr. Octavius had clearly lost control. The four mechanical arms swung wildly about the room, knocking people over, smashing into walls, and tearing the room apart. There was mayhem in the lab!

Spider-Man to the rescue!

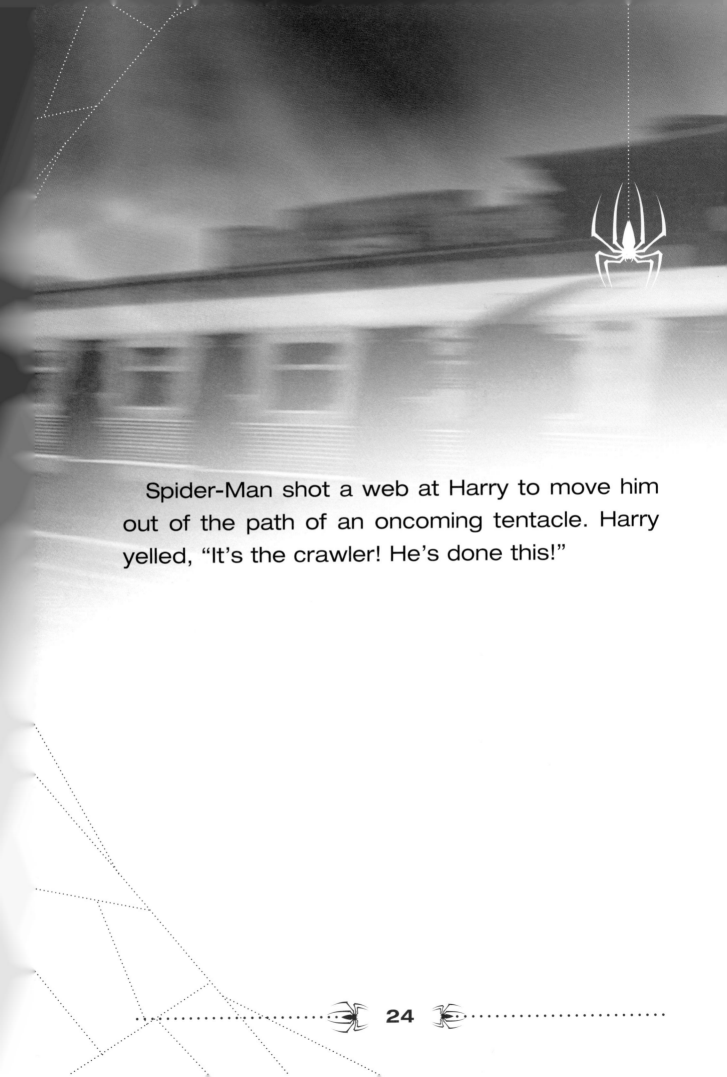

Spider-Man shot a web at Harry to move him out of the path of an oncoming tentacle. Harry yelled, "It's the crawler! He's done this!"

Dr. Octavius's smart arms continued to flail uncontrollably. They crashed into an electrical power supply, sending a current through the arms and up Dr. Octavius's back. He grabbed his head and screamed in agony. The artificial arms were now welded to his body!

The electrical surge continued to pulse through Dr. Octavius's body. Spider-Man rushed over to the power supply to disconnect it. As Spider-Man pulled the plug, Dr. Octavius fell to the floor in a heap, motionless. A moment later, the smart arms rose up in the air as if they had minds of their own.

Later that night, several surgeons stood over the body of Dr. Octavius, laid out on a hospital operating table. They examined the smart arms and discussed how to remove them from Octavius's spine. Then, without warning, the arms came to life and attacked the doctors, hurling them across the room, pinning them to walls, and even choking them.

Afterwards, Dr. Octavius woke up and surveyed the chaos surrounding him. Unconscious bodies were strewn about the floor, and glass jars and vials were shattered, various colored liquids spilling out of them. When he realized he was the cause of the mess, he screamed out in agony and fled.

The doctor wandered through the city and ended up back at his lab. The room was completely destroyed. As he looked around, Dr. Octavius heard the sound of a siren approaching. He realized that the police must be after him. He couldn't stick around here; they would know just where to find him. An old, abandoned pier stood off in the distance. That's where he would go.

He reached the pier and huddled inside a small, dilapidated building at the end of it. What had gone wrong? How did this happen? Dr. Octavius was only sure of one thing: Somehow Spider-Man was to blame. He vowed to get his revenge—and return to his work—whatever the price.

The following day, Peter was passing a bank when his spider sense kicked in. He glanced through the window and spotted a man in a trench coat breaking into the vault. Four menacing tentacles emerged from the man's coat. Dr. Octavius was now Doc Ock—a maniacal monster with eight limbs!

The guards tried to stop him but Doc Ock tossed them aside like rag dolls. He reached into the vault and greedily gathered bags of money and gold coins with his tentacles.

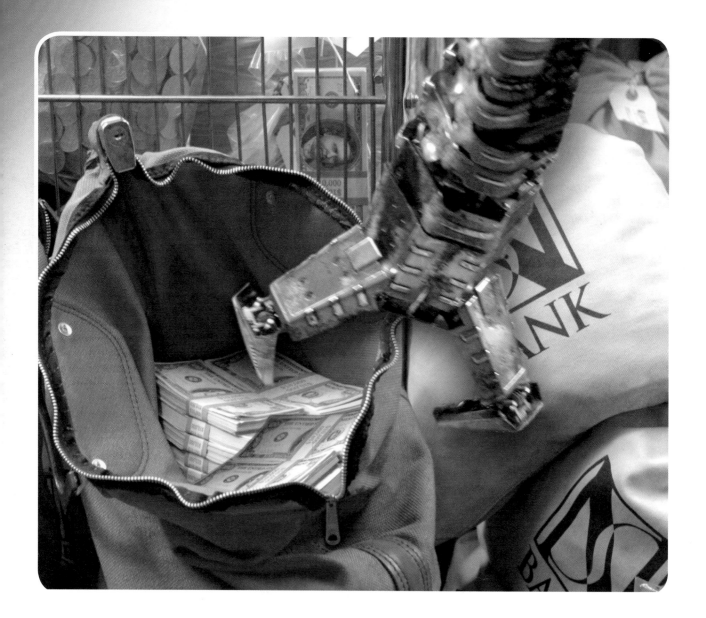

Then Spider-Man swooped in! Doc Ock hurled the heavy bags at Spider-Man, knocking him to the floor. "How dare you interfere with me again!" hissed the madman.

Doc Ock had Spider-Man in a stranglehold! But even as he gasped for breath, Spider-Man webbed a heavy desk. When he yanked it, the desk sailed toward Doc Ock and knocked him through a window and out onto the street.

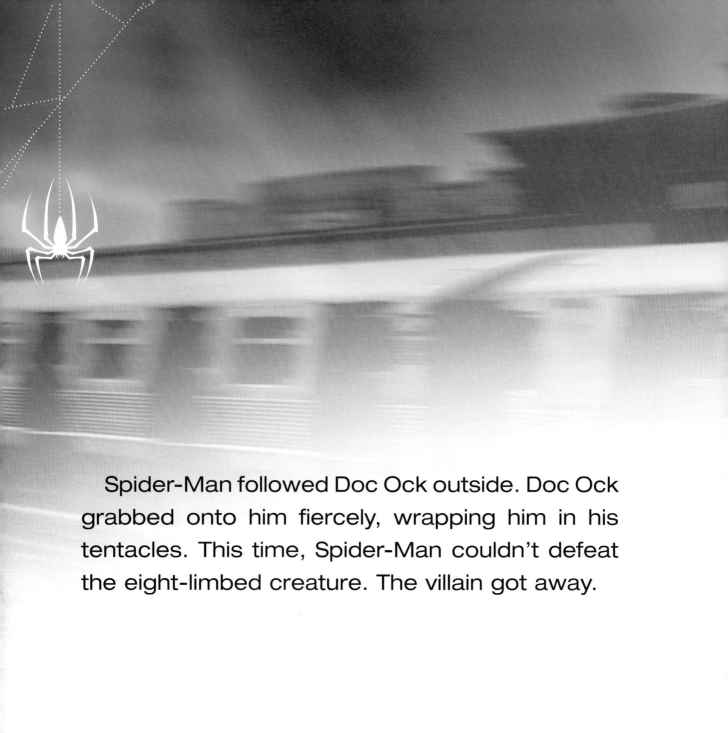

Spider-Man followed Doc Ock outside. Doc Ock grabbed onto him fiercely, wrapping him in his tentacles. This time, Spider-Man couldn't defeat the eight-limbed creature. The villain got away.

Peter arrived back at his apartment, sad and weary. He sat down on his bed and looked around the room. His eyes wandered over photographs of Uncle Ben, Aunt May, and M. J. A pile of overdue bills spilled out over the unopened schoolbooks on his desk. He looked at the crumpled-up Spider-Man suit on the floor and shook his head. "This isn't worth it." He picked up the suit, stuffed it into a box, and shoved it into the back of his closet.

The next day, Peter asked M. J. to meet him at a coffee shop near his apartment. He greeted her with a big smile. "Things are different now, M. J. Things have changed. I'm going to be a better person, a better friend, and someone who can be there for you."

He certainly sounded sincere. M. J. believed his good news. "As part of the new me," Peter went on, "I have to go help Aunt May move some furniture. I'll talk to you later."

Peter arrived at Aunt May's. "Did you get any pictures of Spider-Man battling Doc Ock at the bank?" she asked.

"How do you know about that?" Peter asked. He found out that two of Aunt May's friends had been at the bank and had seen the whole thing. Spider-Man had saved their lives, she explained, and they were so grateful to have him around, helping out their city.

Peter felt his heart swell. Of course. How could he have forgotten that Spider-Man was beloved by the people in this city? Peter knew what he had to do. He couldn't abandon his duties. He had to continue to help people whenever he could. After all, no sacrifice was too great when you were doing something that really mattered.

While Spider-Man had been taking some time off, Doc Ock had been devastating the city. One night, he showed up at Harry Osborn's apartment and demanded money to finish his research.

"No way," said Harry. "I won't give you more money . . . unless, unless . . . you kill Spider-Man."

"Consider it done," replied Doc Ock. "Do you know how to find him?"

"Just look for Peter Parker," Harry said. "He always seems to know where Spider-Man is."

As Peter rode back to the city that night on his motorbike, he felt like he was being followed. All of a sudden, a tentacle swooped down beside him and plucked him off of his bike. Doc Ock pulled Peter close to his face. "Tell Spider-Man to meet me at Pier Fifty-Six or I'll hunt you down and kill you!" Before Peter could say a word, Doc Ock lowered him to the ground and took off.

Peter wasted no time in switching into his Spider-Man costume. Spider-Man swung through the city, ready for his face-off with the mad scientist.

Doc Ock swiped Spider-Man off the pier the minute he arrived. Then he grasped him by the throat and the two fell into combat, tumbling over each other. Doc Ock pummeled Spider-Man with all of his tentacles at once. As Doc Ock wound up for a fatal blow, Spider-Man twisted away and shot a web at him. Finally, Doc Ock and his tentacles were tangled up for good.

Later that night, Peter met M. J. at the coffee shop. He was a little bit late and he noticed she looked at him with disappointment. Maybe he couldn't live up to the promise he had made to be a better friend. In fact, that's why he wanted to meet with her. He had to tell her he couldn't be around as much as he would like to be.

"But is it something you want—for us to be friends?" she asked him.

"Yes," Peter said.

"Then we'll work on it together," M. J. said. "You try harder, and I'll try harder, and we'll meet in the middle."

Peter walked away with a huge smile on his face. He knew he could do it—keep the city safe *and* have a life. After all, he would *always* be Spider-Man.